The Taj Mahal Adventure

When you go on an adventure prepare for the unexpected. You never know what you may find or what may find you! Jay and Juhi know this well. They are master adventurers, but they have their share of surprises. During this particular adventure they visit one of the Seven Wonders of the World! Listen closely, this is an adventure you won't want to miss.

Jay and Juhi were running around the kitchen playing tag when they ran right into Mommy who was carrying a vase to the table.

"Ooooops!"

"Sorry Mommy," Jay and Juhi said as the vase fell to the floor. It broke into two large pieces and one small shiny yellow piece in the shape of a flower.

"How did that painted flower come off so perfectly?" Juhi asked.

"It's not painted; all the designs you see on this marble vase are made from gemstones. The yellow flower is carved from topaz," Mommy said.

"I hope we can fix it," Juhi said sadly.

"Don't worry, we'll try," said Mommy.

Jay and Juhi went to their room to do some investigating and learn more about marble vases.

"Let's look it up in my electronic encyclopedia!" Jay said. He typed in the letters:

M - A - R - B - L - E   V - A - S - E

"Look at all those beautiful vases! That one looks like Mommy's!" Juhi said.

"If we can find out how this vase is made, maybe we can figure out how to fix the broken vase," Jay said. "Are you thinking what I'm thinking?" Jay asked.

"Yes!" Juhi replied as she took her magic flute, Soori, out of a sparkly purple box.

♪♪ **"Soori, Soori with music you know, please take us where we need to go!"** ♪♪

Juhi played a beautiful song on her flute. As she played, there was a magnificent flash of light and they were off—encyclopedia in hand!

"Where do you think we are?" asked Jay. Jay and Juhi looked around. They were on the side of a very busy street.

Suddenly, a large group of kids ran right in front of them. Trying to get out of the way, Jay and Juhi stumbled into a store behind them.

"Whoa!" Jay said losing his balance and falling right into a table holding a marble vase.

"Not again!" said Juhi.

"Don't worry, I got it!" said a boy behind them who caught the vase before it fell.

"That was a close one!" said Jay. "Good catch!"

"Thanks, it's my job to look after things here. This is my family's store. My name is Sameer."

"Hi Sameer, I'm Jay and this is my sister, Juhi."

"I'm happy to meet you, welcome."

"We make and sell parchin kari crafts in our store."

"Parchin . . . what?" Juhi asked.

"Parchin kari," replied Sameer.

"It's also called marble inlay. Artists carve shapes and designs out of marble and then fill them in with specially carved jewels and stones, like rubies and emeralds!"

"Just like Mommy's vase!" Juhi said. "The one we broke."

"Don't worry, you can fix it with special glue," said Sameer.

"What a relief, we'll have to tell Mommy about that," Juhi said.

"I can't believe all this is made of marble!" said Jay looking around the shop.

"You can make a lot out of marble, small crafts like these as well as huge buildings!" said Sameer.

"Buildings?" questioned Juhi in disbelief.

"Sure, haven't you heard of the Taj Mahal? It's made entirely out of pure white marble," Sameer said.

"Yes! I remember reading about it in my encyclopedia," Jay said. "The Taj Mahal is in Agra, India, and it's one of the Seven Wonders of the World!"

"We have to see that someday!" Juhi said.

"How about today? After all, you are in Agra! Come on, I'll take you there. I just have to get one thing before we go," said Sameer as he reached into a desk drawer and grabbed three flashlights.

"What are those for?" Jay asked.

"You'll see," said Sameer. "Come on!"

Jay and Juhi followed Sameer outside.

"Look at this beautiful carriage and horse!"
Juhi exclaimed.

"I'm glad you think so because this is our ride! This is my horse Tongi. I call him that because he gives Tonga rides!" Sameer explained as he climbed into the small front seat, holding the reigns of the horse. "Get in!" he called out to Jay and Juhi.

"How did you learn to ride one of these?" Jay asked.

"I've been riding with my dad for years. Now, I can ride by myself. My horse Tongi knows his way around here. Sometimes we even take tourists for rides around town."

"We're not tourists, we're adventurers!" Juhi said.

"Well then we are off for a great adventure!"
 replied Sameer.

Jay and Juhi were enjoying the Tonga ride when all of a sudden Sameer shouted, "Whoa! Whoa!" Tongi stopped just in time!

Passing in front of them was a grand parade with elephants and camels painted and decorated with jewels. There were musicians playing drums and people singing. Everyone was wearing colorful festive clothes.

It was a spectacular sight!

"What's going on? Is it a special holiday?" Juhi asked. "It's the beginning of a festival called Taj Mahotsav, held every year here in the city of Agra to celebrate the arts, crafts, and culture of our state, Uttar Pradesh."

After the parade passed by, Jay, Juhi, and Sameer continued their ride.

They arrived at an impressive red sandstone gateway.

As they walked through, a grand white marble structure suddenly appeared. The Taj Mahal looked like a palace, but unlike any they had ever seen before.

"Wow" said Jay "It's incredible! I wonder who built this."

"The great emperor Shah Jahan built the Taj Mahal over 300 years ago." Sameer said. "It took 22 years to build, 20,000 workers to help build it, and 1000 elephants to help carry all the building materials!"

"Wow, that's a lot of years, and a lot of people!" exclaimed Juhi.

As they continued to walk, they saw a large pool that reflected a perfect image of the Taj Mahal.

"This pool is like a giant mirror!" Juhi observed.

"Look I can see my reflection," said Jay as he leaned over the side of the pool.

"That's why people call this the reflecting pool. In fact, it's the most famous reflecting pool in the world," Sameer explained.

"I can see why!" said Jay.

"What kind of palace is the Taj Mahal?" asked Juhi.

"It's not a palace, it's actually a tomb," Sameer said in a mysterious voice. "Shah Jahan built it for his wife, Mumtaz Mahal, after she died. He loved her so much that he wanted to build a beautiful place where people could come and remember her."

"So you mean Mumtaz Mahal is buried here?" Jay asked.

"Yes, and so is Shah Jahan," Sameer explained.

"Let's go inside, there's something I want to show you."

"I'm not sure if we need to go inside," said Jay hesitantly.

"Yeah," agreed Juhi, "the outside is so beautiful and. . ."

"Come on," interrupted Sameer as he handed them each a flashlight. "I thought you were adventurers! Let's go!"

Jay and Juhi cautiously followed Sameer into the Taj Mahal. It was darker, but not completely dark. A beautiful lamp created a soft glow inside. It was very peaceful.

Jay and Juhi were amazed by what they saw; they were not scared at all. They saw the two marble tombs side by side behind a marble screen. They saw beautiful and colorful parchin kari designs on the marble archways around them.

"Come this way!" whispered Sameer as he led them to a nearby wall. "Stand here, I'll go to the other side, keep your eyes on the wall!"

Jay and Juhi stood together and watched the wall in front of them, when suddenly they saw a small light moving around on it. "Do you see it?" Sameer asked quietly.

"We do, we do!" whispered Jay and Juhi with excitement. "How are you doing that?"

"With my flashlight!" Sameer responded.

"How can a flashlight shine through a solid wall?" Juhi questioned.

"This marble is translucent," Sameer said.

"Let me look that up," Jay said as he took out his encyclopedia. "This wall is translucent. That means that light can shine through. That's why we saw Sameer's light on our side of the wall."

"Let's try it!" said Juhi. Jay and Juhi shined their flashlights at the wall.

"I see it, I see your lights!" Sameer said.

"Wow! Everything about the Taj Mahal is intriguing!" said Jay.

Jay, Juhi, and Sameer walked back outside to continue their adventure.

"Look, Juhi," said Jay, "there is an orange glow on the dome!"

"That's the sun's reflection, the color of the sunset. In the morning there is a light pinkish glow as the sun comes up. My favorite time to see the Taj Mahal is on a clear night, when the reflection of the moonlight makes it shine even brighter!" Sameer said.

"I wish I could see that!" said Juhi.

"Me too!" Jay agreed. "We will have to come back again one day, but right now we have to get back home."

They took one last look at the Taj Mahal.

Jay and Juhi walked with Sameer back to Tongi.

"Can I give you a ride?" Sameer asked. "No thanks, we have one!" Juhi said.

"Thank you for bringing us to the Taj Mahal, we will never forget it!" said Jay.

"Please come back again soon so we can have another adventure!" Sameer said as he began to drive away. "We will!" Jay and Juhi said, waving goodbye.

"Are you ready?" Jay asked Juhi. "I'm ready!" Juhi took out Soori and called out with Jay:

♪♪ **"Soori, Soori with music you know, please take us where we need to go!"** ♪♪

Juhi began to play a happy song and, in a magnificent flash of light, they went home.

Jay and Juhi walked into the kitchen and saw that Mommy and Daddy had already fixed the vase.

"You fixed the parchin kari vase!" said Juhi in a happy voice. "Did you use a special glue?"

"Yes we did. How did you know it was parchin kari?" asked Daddy. "I learned about it from a friend," replied Juhi.

"Daddy and I got this vase on our first trip together to the Taj Mahal. We hope to take you and Jay there sometime soon." Mommy said.

"I can hardly wait to go back!" exclaimed Juhi.

"Go back?" Mommy asked in a confused voice.

"I mean . . . I can't wait to go there!" Juhi said giggling.

Jay and Juhi smiled. What a wondrous adventure they had had!

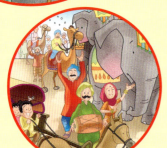

DO YOU REMEMBER?

- What was the event that made Jay and Juhi curious about marble vases?
- Where is the Taj Mahal located?
- How did Sameer transport Jay and Juhi to the Taj Mahal?
- In whose memory was the Taj Mahal built? By whom?
- What was the festival being celebrated in Agra?
- What special quality does marble have?

DID YOU KNOW?

- Shah Jahan and Mumtaz Mahal had 14 children.
- The white marble used to construct the Taj Mahal, was brought from Makrana in Rajasthan India.
- 28 different kinds of semi-precious stones were used in the inlay work in the Taj Mahal. These included Turquoise from Tibet, Sapphires from Sri Lanka and Lapis Lazuli from Afghanistan.
- It is the white marble and semi-precious stones on the dome of the Taj that make Taj Mahal change color during the day and on moonlit nights.
- The area around the Taj Mahal is a pollution free zone, so no diesel or gasoline driven vehicles are allowed.
- When translated in English Taj Mahal means 'Crown Palace' or 'Crown of the Palace'.
- The Hindi word for the inlay work is pachchikaree but in English it is often referred to as parchinkari.

DO IT YOURSELF!

Make a parchin kari vase.

You will need: A plastic bottle, white paint, colored paper and glue.

1. Paint the plastic bottle white.
2. Cut the colored paper into small diamond, square, triangle and circle shapes (to mimic gemstones).
3. Once the paint has dried on the bottle, glue the "gemstones" on the bottle to make an interesting design.

Your vase is ready!

Continue your adventure with Jay and Juhi at www.MeeraMasi.com